His to

By Genni Bee

Author's Note

Hey readers,

You're about to read one of my steamy novellas, complete with very mature situations, curse words, some mild stalking danger and more than a few uses of the word cock.

If you are here for the spice and an almost-instalove romance…this is the right book for you.

All the best,

Genni Bee

Chapter 1

Hannah

I couldn't remember another time in my entire life that I had been more nervous. Except for that night, a few weeks ago, when I'd sat on my childhood bathroom floor holding the deciding factor of my future in my hands and praying.

But that path was now chosen, surer than anything else in my tumultuous life. Today my nerves were centered around one person.

A man, actually. Declan Windham.

The very man who I hoped was about to be my new employer, and therefore the unassuming hero in my fairytale gone wrong. Anxiety bloomed fresh under my ribs, making my breath come short in tired lungs. Looking down, I forced a deep breath, focusing on how the oxygen forced its way into my body, expanding my chest, quieting my mind. But not enough. I could hear the voices on the other side of the wall get louder. Closer.

When the door swung open, my eyes instantly flickered up to meet the dark, serious green eyes of Declan Windham. Once there, I was frozen, unable to look away.

With a nod to his companion, the man approached me, his broad shoulders shifting under the deep navy suit that outlined a form which was proof of the man's fitness. His skin was fair, a sharp contrast to his close-cropped dark hair. His cheeks were adorned with what looked to be a perfectly designed five o'clock shadow.

I'd never enjoyed dating someone with any kind of scruff. I typically found it unkempt, making me think of a lazy ex-boyfriend. The way Declan Windham wore it had me wondering why I had ever dared to think otherwise, because every intimidating inch of him screamed polish.

Subconsciously, I turned in on myself, my battered black heels suddenly too scuffed and old to be in the same time zone as this man. I swallowed audibly; my eyes still trapped by his. Mr. Windham must've seen my panic, because his handsome face softened a fraction, the dimple in his cheek winking as he offered a small smile.

"Ms. Palazzo?" He reached out, his large, calloused hand enclosing mine. With a soft tug, I found myself drawn up and closer to the man. His cologne hit me, the pine scent of his skin swirling into my brain, parting the fog of nerves as I steadied myself before him.

"It's nice to meet you, Mr. Windham, sir," I said softly, afraid to tear my gaze away. His hand still held mine, the skin warm. For the first time in weeks, something in me relaxed, sighed, taking in the man's easy authority.

"Declan will do fine. Come on in." Declan's hand released mine, and I instantly missed that steadying warmth. Ducking my chin, I followed him obediently into his office. I had to choke back the noise that threatened as I looked around his executive suite. It would fit the entire apartment I'd just signed the lease on. And then some.

Then again, Declan Windham was a partner in the uber-successful legal firm of Calvin, Windham and Rayne. I was a twenty-one-year-old night school student who had just found out she had a very significant life change coming her way.

We were not the same.

For some reason, that hurt more than I expected, and a single sniff slipped out. I coughed over it, attempting to hide the tangle of emotions. These hormones would be the death of me. If Mr. Windham noticed, he didn't say anything. I continued to follow the dark shadow of his body as we moved towards his desk.

Against one wall was a multitude of pictures, large enough that I could see a common thread in all of them. They were families, each with the same darked, angular-faced boy alongside them. I squinted, attempting to see more detail.

There was no other art on the walls, making this gallery important. At least to the man in the office. I hurried to catch up as he cleared his throat.

"I hope you weren't waiting long."

I shook my head quickly. "Not at all. I don't mind."

"Before we begin, do you have any questions for me?" One green eye casually observed me as he glanced back over his shoulder.

"I, uh…" My tongue was suddenly thick in my mouth.

The internet had told me that Mr. Windham was a single man who had graduated top of his class, spending several years as a public defender before joining forces with two of his close friends to found their own firm. Ten odd years later, their firm stood tall among the others in the city. Clients loved them. Employees loved them.

When my friend Stephanie had called, practically screaming about how her father's friend was looking for a new assistant, I had jumped at the opportunity. One resume, a flurry of email correspondence, and suddenly I was here in the elaborate offices, waiting to be interviewed.

And I needed a job. Badly. Especially after everything that had happened in the past few weeks. Declan's shadow slowed, and I jerked my chin up, nearly running into his back. I cringed away, afraid of somehow creasing the beautifully tailored suit that he wore.

He must've thought I was falling, as he turned quickly, hands catching my elbow firmly. "Are you alright, Ms. Palazzo?"

"Yes." My cheeks flamed. "Sorry about that, sir."

Under his touch, even through the borrowed black blazer, I could feel the gentle strength in his hands. I didn't dare look up to meet his eyes again. Butterflies took flight somewhere deep in my gut.

He released me. "Please, take a seat."

I obeyed, dropping onto the edge of a plush sofa and quickly crossing my legs at the ankles. I pushed my shoes as far under the edge of the seating as I could, relieved that he seemed to be distracted by his own clothing to notice my antics.

"Thank you for meeting with me on such short notice, Mr. Windh—Declan, I mean."

He was settling himself in a simple black chair facing me. His dark head bowed as he unbuttoned his suit jacket.

Between us, I recognized my resume on the table, but he didn't reach for it. Instead, he pinned me with another curious look, giving me more time to admire his face.

He was impossibly attractive. And not just all slashing cheekbones and perfect dimples. The air that swirled between us, around him, it was a commanding air of authority that should've intimidated me, save the softness of his lips. If I had any cash to spare, I would've bet that he had a lovely smile. Maybe someday I would get to see it.

"Can I ask why you wanted to move the interview up?"

You mean, why am I so desperate to start this job? How do you say "my parents are kicking me out because I alerted them to the presence of their first grandchild" in corporate speak?

I squirmed on the sofa. "My roommates have informed me of a change in living situation. The new apartment I'd like to lease requires more consistent employment." Red-hot embarrassment threatened to turn my entire body pink as those knowing eyes swept over me once more.

"Understandable." Then his lips quivered, ever so slightly. "I've not had roommates in a long time, but I remember it always being quite chaotic."

I laughed, not just because I could never see Declan Windham sharing his living quarters with something as normal as a roommate. But also because of the continued insanity of referring to my parents as roommates.

"It was unexpected to say the least. But I will figure something out. I always do." Concentrate, Hannah, I reminded myself sternly, forcing a polite smile back to my face.

Declan's response surprised me. His hands rolled into fists, his knuckles white against the dark fabric of his slacks. Even the muscle in his jaw leapt as he glared into the rug below his feet.

"Declan, have I done something wrong?"

He didn't seem to hear me. Or decided to flat-out ignore me. "Your resume was impressive, and I spoke with your supervisors at Laurent Engineering. They had nothing but wonderful things to say about you, even when you were part-time."

I ducked my chin. "That's very kind of them. I enjoyed my time there."

Declan leaned back in his chair, strong thighs parted, and he resettled his hands against them. His elegant fingers wrapped around the muscle there.

I glued my eyes to the contrast of his bright shirt to the darkness of his lapel. Anything to not look down and wonder. Or stare. Or freaking drool at this point. I was no better than a common catcalling bro on the streets.

Internally I cringed and pressed a hand against my belly. Those butterflies had progressed to full-size dragons at this point.

"You should know that I really brought you in today to formally offer you the position as my assistant."

My hands flew to my face, shock and relief making my head light. But Declan kept talking, his face serious.

"Wait, Miss Palazzo. There's one more thing. This case is for the university on the outskirts of town. Many days it makes more sense to work from my home office. I'd like to be sure that you are comfortable working out of my home as well."

My eyes burned, confusion warring in my chest. Excitement and anxiety swirled together. "Your house?"

What would the people here think of me? It would be so easy to suppose that I'd jumped into bed with the powerful law firm partner. I bit my lip as anxiety washed over me.

"Before you get worried, there's nothing unusual about it. Lydia, my former assistant, often worked alongside me at home. Plus whoever else from the firm was accompanying me that day. You will have an office and desk at both locations. It's very professional."

"Oh." That didn't seem bad at all. A small, curious bit of my mind woke, excited to see what kind of home a man like Declan lived in. "That won't be a problem at all. I'm sure the address will be provided."

Declan nodded. "Of course, everything will be set. If you desire, a car service can be set up should the drive be too long to your new apartment."

"You don't need to do that. That's too much."

"I do." His voice accepted no other response, so I stared up at him, helpless to the throb and clench deep in my belly as those sinful lips quirked in a ghost of a smile. "I take care of my people, Ms. Palazzo. And as of now, that includes you."

***

Chapter 2

Declan

I was going to murder Rayne.

He'd opened his goddamned mouth, and now instead of using his sensible but prickly assistant Tyler, I was staring down the one and only candidate for my personal assistant job.

And she was gorgeous.

Her resume claimed she was twenty-one, making her nearly twenty years my junior. Hannah was working hard to finish her last few months on school online. She came with an impeccable background of contract work, a sweet smile, and a body that would tempt any man within a ten-mile radius.

And let's not even get into the sweetness of her voice. It washed over me, cleansing my stresses, washing my worries away with a few uttered words and the flash of a brilliant smile.

Something buried deep in my chest had come to life then. Something I hadn't considered in years. That I barely dared to think about.

I wanted her.

But that was a moot point, wasn't it? Because I'd just hired the girl, making her officially off-limits. What kind of stupid move was that? But the minute she'd looked up at me, cheeks flushed and nervous when she talked about the new home she wanted for herself... I would've given her anything. A job, the apartment she wanted—hell, she could come sleep right next to me in the master suite at my house. In fact, I'd rather that than anything else.

I groaned silently, shifting in my chair as my cock took a shine to the idea of that beauty stretched out beside me.

"Do you have any other questions for me?" Her hands were clenched nervously in front of her body. I glanced down as subtly as I could. No ring. It shouldn't have sent a thrill over my body, but it did. I took a deep, rattling breath, trying to calm the pounding in my blood.

"Tell me something about yourself. We'll be working together a significant portion of the day, every day. I'd love to know more."

Her eyes shone like pure golden sunshine as she danced around my request. "I'm not very interesting, Declan."

"I'm sure you are. You can tell me anything." I was suddenly insistent, hoping that she would divulge something personal. I craved the thought of getting to know more about her. To know everything about her, from the sweet curve of her thigh to what her favorite color was. I wanted it all. Needed it, in fact.

Hannah leaned back, hands pressed between her knees as her pencil skirt inched up, another slim expanse of skin bared to my eyes. Like a starving man, I devoured it. And would've begged for more if her words had not followed. "Hmm. I was a competitive swimmer in high school. I love to read, mostly historical romances. And my favorite food is sushi."

I couldn't help the smile that peeked out, curling my lips as I watched her. "We have more in common than you might think."

She smiled back, her face still bright. "Which part? I find it rather hard to picture you reading historical romances…"

I laughed, the sound deep and surprising to not just her. But it felt good, that loose warmth that kept filling my chest. "Ms. Palazzo, you are—"

My door swung open, slicing through the flirtatious atmosphere and throwing a proverbial ice bucket over my shoulders.

"Mr. Windham, I'm sorry to interrupt but your two o'clock is here. Rayne is already waiting in the conference room."

I glared daggers at the slender man, his notebook and phone neatly stacked in his hands. Rayne's assistant was top notch but clearly had no idea what he had just interrupted.

"Great, Tyler, thank you," I gritted out as I stood slowly.

Hannah stayed seated, and unless I was mistaken, her face was tainted with the same disappointment that filled mine.

Tyler's delightful interruptions apparently were not complete. Smiling, he gestured to Hannah. "Would you want me to walk your guest out?"

I ground my teeth. "Thank you, Tyler, I will walk Ms. Palazzo out."

Tyler turned to leave, when her voice stopped him. "Excuse me, Tyler, was it? Wait just one moment."

Hannah rose off the sofa, her tightly fitted black skirt sliding higher as she did. I jerked my head to Tyler's, fully prepared to snarl if the man looked anywhere south of her collarbones. To his credit, the man seemed blissfully unaware of the magnitude of beauty that we shared the room with.

"You don't have to do that, Mr. Windham. I will sneak out this way so you won't be late to your next meeting." She plucked up her bag. "After all, I will be seeing you soon. Right?"

"Right, Miss Palazzo." I stood stiffly, allowing her to join Tyler with a soft smile of greeting. Her nerves seem to have abated, but there was something about her that called out to me, fragile and delicate. I wanted to reach out, to wrap myself around her and make sure nothing bad could happen to her ever again.

I clamped my jaw shut, refusing to relinquish all control to the caveman inner voice I had suddenly acquired. "I'm looking forward to working with you, Miss Palazzo."

Just as she reached the door, her lovely face tilted back to me. "Goodbye, Declan." In a soft voice, almost a whisper, she added, "You should call me Hannah."

Then with a flash of long, fair legs and black fabric, she vanished from my office.

My hands curled into fists. I was ready to track down Samuel Rayne. And then murder him. Twice.

First, Sam insinuated I needed a new assistant and he had the perfect candidate. He made sure that I saw her and would clearly find her maddingly attractive. Then the nosy bastard sent his assistant to escort her out. What a joke.

As soon as Hannah and Tyler were out of earshot, I reached for the recessed door that led to the combined conference room between Sam's office and my own.

"What the hell are you trying to do to me?"

My longtime friend and business partner didn't bat an eye. "Good afternoon, sunshine. How are you?"

"Don't play the clown. You know what you did." I stormed across to the liquor cabinets, which were always stocked with our favorites. Today it was scotch. Something smooth that could wash away the fact that I was about to spend every day across a desk from the woman I wanted the most.

I splashed some into a glass, still cursing.

Sam's brown eyes sparkled. "Safe to say you met your new assistant?"

I growled, throwing the liquor down my throat with ease. After slamming the glass down, I approached the table again, glaring. Smug bastard was still smiling at me, so I knew he didn't actually need or desire an answer. I plopped down in the chair opposite him.

"I'll take that as a yes. Good for you, Windham. She's perfect for the job. And Stephanie, Gregory's daughter, only has great things to say. Maybe now you can leave Tyler the fuck alone so I can get something accomplished."

"I offered her the job. She will start as soon as human resources clears her." My temper ebbed, my vision clearing as I faced my friend.

Sam was leaning towards me on his elbows, his chin resting on one large fist. His Vanderbilt ring flashed from his knuckles. While we had come from very different upbringings, there was no one else I was closer to. Most days I considered the man like a brother, along with the third founding partner of our company, Jamie Calvin.

Sam gave him a hard look. "What's got you all riled up? I thought you would be grateful; I practically served the woman up on a platter. You know that Jamie would've taken her in an instant. He's looking too."

I growled, my fingers clenching on the glass. "She's mine."

"Okay, fine. So, what's the deal? You look like you're ten seconds from a meltdown, man." Realization dawned, sharp and clear on his face. Sam's body folded over the table, glee across every line in his face. "Oh shit. You like your new assistant."

I crossed my arms. "I already said I did. I offered her the job."

But Sam must've smelled the blood in the water. His voice rose as he moved around the table to prop a hip next to me. "It's more than that."

"I don't know what you're talking about."

"The girl. Oh God, you like her." Sam thrust his hands into the air, triumphant. "I can't believe that the man of stone has a crack." He twisted to look at me. "Now I wish I'd come by the interview. Is she pretty? Did you ask her out? What was she wearing?"

I growled again, my blood beginning to pound. "Leave it alone, Sam."

"I will not. I've waited years—years, Declan—to find you somebody. And while I didn't mean for that somebody to be your new assistant, what can I say? Two birds, one stone."

"Don't talk about her like that."

"Protective already? Did you ask her out?"

"No, she's my assistant, and she needs the job. I can't ask her out and ruin that." The truth tasted metallic against my tongue. But Sam was relentless.

"Pish, posh. Whose name is on the outside of this building. We can make exceptions. Especially for you, Declan. It's been too long since you've had someone special."

My glass was empty, but I didn't dare drink more. Not when I was already so rattled. I cracked my knuckles with a sigh. "You're incorrigible."

"Great vocab word. Ten points to you. Now, when are you seeing her next?"

"I told you, whenever human resources clear her through security."

Sam drummed on the polished wood table. "You know what's something she could do without security clearances?"

"What?"

"Go on a date with you."

"Fuck you, man. Don't rush me."

"Rush you? You haven't seen anybody in years. It would be good for you. And based on what Stephanie told me, the girl could use some good in her life too." Sam moved away, nonchalantly twirling his pen.

But still, I shifted, intrigued. "What do you mean?"

"Her parents have been threatening to kick her out for months, and I think they are finally doing it. That's why she's switching to online to finish up her degree."

Her roommates—or, apparently, her parents—were kicking her out. I remembered the embarrassment that she'd shown that vulnerability. Suddenly things made even more sense for the lovely Hannah. I rubbed a hand over my chest where that pesky ache continued on.

"She can get her new place now. That's great too, right?" Sam's voice was low. He knew what dangerous territory we were in.

"Absolutely. Any parent who doesn't take care of their child in need doesn't deserve to have them anyway."

Sam offered a smile, opening up his laptop. He knew my history well. "I couldn't agree more. Now, before Tyler comes back in here to kick my ass, can we get this amendment figured out?"

"Yeah, sure." I leaned in, nodding and mumbling responses as Sam made his recommendations. But my mind was already elsewhere, trapped in a world where nobody could ever hurt Hannah Palazzo. The idea was not only interesting, but addicting, and the more I thought about it, the more I wanted to be the one to make it happen.

***

Chapter 3

Hannah

My first day at Calvin, Windham and Rayne started off going as smooth as I ever could've asked for. I found the parking lot on the first try. My identification card picture didn't look too awful. And the girl sitting next to me at orientation was friendly and kind. And most importantly, I'd somehow managed to do all of this without letting it slip that was I was almost three months pregnant.

But the easy part was behind me. I was on my way to find my desk outside of the executive suites. Or rather, Declan's office. I gnawed on my lower lip, the hand on the edge of my purse growing damp with another surge of nervousness.

What if he asked me to do something I didn't know how to do?

What if I messed up one of his big cases?

What if I got fired? I couldn't get fired now. I needed this job. I needed it so badly. We both did. I pressed my hand against my belly, trying to calm my thoughts and my heart rate. Barely succeeding, I moved down the hallway, knowing a trail of curious eyes in my wake.

From what I'd gathered, Lydia, Mr. Windham's last assistant, had been a beloved colleague who only left the company when her family moved across the country. I was nobody but the new girl and following in some enormous footprints.

The dark wood edging signaled the beginning of the executive suites. Gathering my wits, I pushed forward, giving a small wave at Tyler Wiggins, another of the partner's assistants. He waved back, gesturing to the headset that was perched on his blond hair. I nodded, understanding he couldn't come chat right now.

Someone had changed out Lydia's desk tags and replaced them with shining, beautiful nameplates with my own name on them. Excitement bubbled up in my chest, and smiling, I ran a finger along the metal edge. My first real job.

"Ms. Palazzo?" a deep voice asked from behind me.

I gasped, tearing my finger away and leaving a long, slender cut against my index finger. "Mr. Windham, good morning," I stuttered, tucking my finger behind my back.

He was dressed in black today. For the first time, I noticed the dusting of silver. For a moment, I was shocked again at how attractive he was. I'd thought that maybe when I came in last week for my interview that I'd allowed my fantasies to take control, to alter what the man really looked like.

But I was wrong. He was still distractingly good-looking, all hard angles and rough lines. Except for those lips. They were too full, too soft. They didn't belong to a man like him but at the same time fit into the entire persona. As I watched, the tip of a pink tongue swept out to wet them. There was an answering throb deep in my belly.

There was no denying it, no matter how hard I had tried after my interview. I had a thing for my new boss.

I wrenched my eyes back up to meet his, hoping he didn't guess I was thinking about him. Worried that it would change everything. Terrified to let him realize how badly I needed this job. I couldn't keep fantasizing about him. No more drooling over my new boss. Not when I needed to focus on making this successful. I was on my own now. That needed to be a priority.

"Good morning. Do you like the nameplates? I thought they might make you feel more comfortable."

"They are lovely," I answered, a little breathless. I smiled, again hoping he would be too distracted to notice my staring or my hand.

His dark brows lowered, and he took another few steps towards me. "Did you hurt yourself, Ms. Palazzo?"

He was wearing that cologne again, the one that smelled like pine and wind-whipped winters. I breathed him in, even as I tucked the hand farther behind my back. "It's just a little paper cut, sir. No need to worry about it."

Declan's face went dark. An instant later, strong hands pulled my hand out from behind my back and exposed the slender wound to the lights above us. I held my breath as he leaned over my hand, cradling my injury like it was a bullet hole instead of a tiny paper cut.

Warmth spread up my hand, spearing my chest with a sharpness that made my heart do a double take.

"It is my job to worry about you."

My intake of breath must've given me away, telling him exactly how close to home those words hit. "That's very nice, but really, it's okay."

"Come in here. I have a first aid kit at my desk." Declan turned, his hand still holding mine as he ushered me into his office and guided me to the sofa once more.

"That's not necessary. I feel silly."

"You shouldn't. Like I said, it's my job to take care of you." Declan slipped behind his heavy desk, and I could hear the drawers opening and closing as he located a bright-blue first aid kit and brought it back to me.

Instead of sitting next to me or even across from me, the tall man suddenly dropped to a knee in front of me, his warmth and smell immediately enveloping me once more. I sighed, letting my worries slip away as he took my hand in his again, eyeing the cut.

"We are a family here. We take care of our employees. You don't need to hide your pain or injuries—or even concerns— from us. Especially from me." He selected a Band-Aid, squeezed a small amount of ointment onto the gauze portion, and began to wrap it around my injured fingers. "You and I, we are going to be partners. No secrets."

"No secrets," I echoed, surprised at how I sounded as my heart pounded in my ears. The urge to tell him everything, every detail, every pain—it consumed me. And when his warm gaze found mine, I had to physically clamp my lips shut to keep my confessions inside, where they circled, angry and desperate. Instead I blurted out the first thing that came to mind. "The pictures on your wall? Who are they?"

Declan's face was downcast, so I couldn't tell what if he reacted or not. The hand against my own continued to be gentle as he nimbly applied a small stretch of medical tape. "They are all me. One for each of my foster families who helped raise me."

But again, Declan surprised me by holding up my finger for his final approval. Then his eyes focused on my face as he brought my finger closer and then pressed a soft kiss against the injured finger. Again, my body hummed in pleasure, the clenching between my thighs proof of exactly how much I found myself enjoying his attention.

"Thank you," I whispered.

"My pleasure." Declan stood, moving back to his desk quickly, where he sat down, his hand already busy with the stacks of information that covered his desk. "I'd appreciate you sitting in on our afternoon meetings to take minutes and keep us on track. Feel free to spend the morning wrapping up whatever is left from orientation."

Whatever heat had pulsed between us was vanquished by his easy dismissal. I stood stiffly, the change in emotions giving me whiplash. "Of course, Mr. Windham."

I made it all the way to the door before he spoke again, his voice gentle but firm. "When it's just us, Hannah, I'd like you to continue to call me Declan."

I didn't turn, afraid he might see the blush that warmed my cheeks. "Of course, Declan. Let me know if you need anything else." I pushed through the door and into the mercifully cool office space. I was going to need some serious practice dealing with my new boss. Otherwise, I'd find myself becoming a complete puddle every time we had a conversation. And while I knew that was dangerous, I couldn't deny the temptation of doing exactly that.

***

Declan

The fact that the woman who had consumed my every waking and sleeping thought was sitting directly outside my office doors was doing nothing for my productivity. And this morning, when I'd seen her hiding that little cut from me, I'd never felt anything quite like that. The need to help her overrode anything else. Drawing her into my office, holding her hand, wrapping the injury… It had been like a balm on my own wounds. As if healing her might heal my own scarred self.

And the sweetness of her smile when I'd told her I'd take care of her, it had robbed me of all thought. That's why I had practically sprinted back across the room. To hide behind my desk and put it between us. As if the piece of furniture would keep the need to hold her, to pull her close, away.

Well, it hadn't.

Because it had been hours since she went back to her desk, and I could still feel the rush of my blood every time I thought about her.

Sam was right. I was lonely. I did need somebody. But why did my interest have to be piqued by this woman? My brain immediately supplied the answers in a rush.

Because she is kind.

Because she is sweet.

Because she is beautiful.

Because there is something there, simmering between us, that calls to the deepest part of you to protect her.

I was pretty sure that none of these were passing thoughts but were truths that I needed to learn to live with.

The telltale ding on my computer screen alerted me to an urgent email. I passed weary eyes over the message, sighing. Another hurdle in the day, but at least this one I could handle professionally.

I opened the door, speaking just loud enough that Hannah could hear me but no louder. "Hannah, can you please reschedule my afternoon? I need to run home for materials and then possible meetings with the university."

"Do you want me to come with you?"

I shook my head. "That's very kind of you to offer, but no. I'll stay and take my meetings from there."

To my surprise, Hannah's lips formed a firm line. She rose and began to collect her things. "Why don't I come with you, then? I'd like to go over the directions for next time anyway."

I mulled over the thoughts. Originally, I'd been grateful for the moment to gather my wits away from her. But there was no part of me that could resist the sweetness of her voice now. Or the earnest way she looked up at me.

"Okay, sounds like a plan. We'll head out in fifteen."

The smile she sent my way warmed my chest and quickened my step as I turned and moved back into my office. We had a drive ahead of us, and I needed to get my head on straight before I spent that time pinned in the back of a car with the one person I wanted more than anything else.

And I was used to getting what I wanted.

Why was I stopping myself?

Putting my thoughts aside, I threw together everything I would need to work from home this afternoon. Opening the door, I was met with Hannah waiting patiently by her desk, her fingers wrapped tightly around her own laptop bag.

I wanted to take it from her but stilled my fingers. Based on the way she was holding it, it seemed like that was not something she would appreciate. I had built my business because of my ability to read situations. And in this one, I needed to give her space.

Stepping up beside her, I held a hand out, ushering her out the room. "The car will meet us out front. Do you have everything?"

"I do." She nodded, her red-gold hair shimmering forward over one shoulder. I gritted my teeth, forcing my hands to remain attached to the bags I held.

"You lead the way," I said with a curt nod.

Her eyes, so wide and trusting, crinkled as she started off. Hopelessly, I fell into step. As we passed Sam's door, I noticed it was open, and as we passed, the man himself appeared at the entryway. One glance at Hannah, and Declan was completely ready to take out his best friend.

"We'll be back." I shoved the man back into his office. His face was laughing, happy as he toppled back, allowing me this moment. Even Tyler was watching us closely from his desk near Hannah's.

She was beautiful. It was no surprise that men were looking. But I was overwhelmed with the need to make sure everyone knew that she was with me.

She was mine. Or she would be soon. There was no other way. I stepped forward, laying a careful hand at the small of her back and simply supporting her there, all the way out of the building and outside into the Chicago spring.

***

Chapter 4

Hannah

I'd never been chauffeured around before. At least not like this. I'd taken some car-sharing rides home from the smattering of nights that I managed to get out with my friends. But since I'd spent most of my college career making sure that I was working enough to keep myself enrolled, those nights were few and far between.

This was total luxury. The plush leather seats, gently heating the backs of my legs as I settled into the comfort. And beside me, his thigh only inches from mine, sat Declan. He looked every inch the powerful lawyer, completely at ease in this luxury, his long legs crossed at the knee, iPad open on his lap.

I peeked up at his face, my phone still open and scrolling. "How long does it typically take you to get into town every day?"

Declan looked at me. "Actually, I have an apartment in the building adjacent to the firm. My home in the suburbs is where I prefer to be, but the drive in every day makes it difficult, even when someone drives so I can work."

"That makes sense."

"Where is your new place?"

"Only a few minutes from the downtown office. But I don't mind the drive out to the suburbs."

His face was serious as he regarded me. "I think I'll set up a car service for the first few days we are working out there. If the university continues to send us more work, there's a chance we'll be there often. I want you to be comfortable coming back and forth and being able to rest."

I giggled, feeling slightly light-headed at the idea that this would be a regular thing. "I promised myself I would turn you down, but I'll be honest, this is really very nice. I could appreciate that extra hour of time." I pointed a finger at him teasingly. "But only at first. My car will do just fine after that."

"Sure." I could see on his face that he wasn't convinced. And while I wanted to push back and resist, I found his offer both appealing and charming. Something deep in me screamed to take a step back. That this was what had happened with Brandon and it had left me pregnant and utterly alone.

Yet, at the same time, something was different this time. Maybe it was the way he looked at me. Or the way his every breath drew me in. There was something between us, an invisible tether tugging Declan and me ever closer. To what, I wasn't sure. But there was nothing I could do except to hold on and hope for the best.

We both went back to our electronics, me to my email, him to his contracts. And for a while the silence of the car was soothing, comforting. But then the white noise hit me, I could feel it filling my mind, slowing my thoughts. And before I knew any better, my head was bobbing, nodding. I tried to resist the pull, to avoid the inevitable sleep that tugged at me, but it was so hard. Especially when a strong hand turned my chin, tucking me against warm fabric and holding me there.

I nestled in, surrounded by pine trees and snowdrifts. Sighing, I let myself dream.

***

Declan

Things were going well. Not only had Hannah accepted my offer to let my car service retrieve her and bring her safely to my house, but she was finally comfortable enough in my presence that she had relaxed.

I'd seen the shadows flickering across her beautiful face, the edge of tiredness in her eyes. And only a few minutes from the office, she had succumbed completely to the sleep that she clearly needed.

I was quickly becoming addicted to the feeling of being near her. The gentle press of her temple against my shoulder was enough for now. But like a starving man, I wasn't sure how much longer I could resist touching her in return. Especially when her delicate hand lingered between our thighs on the seat, her fingers open and extended as if awaiting another.

Too soon, the car turned into my drive, and the change in road must've finally jostled her awake. Her fingers moved first, clenching, moving, again as if searching. I resisted the urge to slip my fingers there, to press her palm to my lips.

"We're here, Hannah," I said instead, watching as her wide blue eyes flickered open, completely focused on me. Then she blinked sleepily, sending a straight shot of need straight to my cock, where it stayed, insistent. I could picture seeing her like that every day, in my bed, her lips parted and swollen from my kisses, her body relaxed as I pulled her closer.

Fuck.

I was never going to be able to get out of this car now. I pressed my briefcase down across my lap and the raging erection I knew was there.

"I'm sorry. I must've dozed." Her lovely voice was even better now, the low, gravelly quality making me think of nights at home or long, lingering touches in the morning.

I cleared my throat. "Not a problem. You didn't even snore."

Her hand flew to her chest, pressing there as if she were truly horrified. I almost laughed at her plight. "Oh God, I hope not! I was up late packing and just got so comfortable."

"I'm glad you got some rest. It might be a bit of a late night."

"I'm up for it, I promise."

So was I, apparently. I was saved from having to reply as the driver opened Hannah's door. Her face brightened as she gathered her things and allowed him to help her from the sedan.

Taking a deep breath and praying to the gods of temptation that there wouldn't be any more accidental touches between Hannah and me. At least not until I figured out how I was going to make my move…and convince her that she was supposed to be with me.

"Your home is lovely," Hannah murmured softly at my side.

We were just inside the foyer, and I had to admit, her words filled me with a sort of pride I hadn't felt in a long time. Followed quickly by a lurking stab of worry. I'd built this house for one reason. And in a savage turn of fate, it had been left mostly vacant.

"Do you live alone?"

"I do. There is a driver on staff and a cook who stops in to help prepare my meals when I need it, but otherwise it's just me."

Hannah moved into the space, her chin raised as she looked around the rooms. I didn't doubt that she was trying to figure out why a single man, freshly turned forty, had an enormous house full of empty rooms.

I had had plans. And those had been ruined. I wasn't ready to figure out how to explain my failures to her. When I turned back to her, her face was oddly pale.

"Mr. Windham, I feel like an idiot asking this. But are you married? I feel so silly."

"No, Hannah, there's no one else. There hasn't been for a long time." I took a deep breath. "I was engaged many years ago. I bought this house thinking it would show her how badly I wanted this life. The kids, the house, the entire picket fence. And now it stands here as a reminder of what I never managed to acquire."

The words came out rawer than I intended. I didn't dare look at her. I didn't want to witness the pity in her eyes. Her more than anyone else.

Her fingers were smooth, cool as they slipped around my fist, giving it a gentle squeeze. I turned, looking over my shoulder at her. "I understand completely, Declan. And I think any woman who looked at you and ever doubted your devotion was a fool."

I stared at her, my heart in my throat. She was close enough I could smell her perfume. Rose petals, sweet and delicate, exactly like the woman who wore them.

No doubt feeling the tension between us, Hannah suddenly ducked her chin, her fingers leaving mine as she stepped away to move towards the hall to my offices, stopping at a photograph on the wall. "Are these all the firm's owners?"

I shook myself, attempting to right my mind. "That's all of us when we met. Samuel Rayne, the chatterbox. Jamie Calvin, the power."

She looked back at me, her lips pulling into a smile. "And Declan Windham… What were you? The money?"

I shook my head.

She tilted her head. "The inspiration?"

I moved closer, compelled by the way her eyes went wide and dark as I drew closer. "Try again," I commanded, my voice low and quiet.

"The…" She leaned back, staring up at me as I grew ever closer. Close enough that I could see the beautiful little green flecks in her eyes as she stared up at me. "The leader?" she guessed, her voice practically a whisper.

I leaned down, my body throbbing with her closeness, and pressed a hand against her side. "I'm the determination, sweet Hannah."

Her breathing was ragged as I leaned in, letting my nose slip over her shoulder as I soaked in the sweetness of her smell, the tangy flavor that it felt like across my tongue. More than anything, I longed to compare it to the real thing. To what it meant to have Hannah completely.

"The determination," she repeated. Slowly, ever so slowly, her hands rose, as if of their own accord, to press against the lapels of my suit.

"Yes," I gritted out. "I always go after what I want."

"Always," she murmured, her fingers tracing designs against my chest.

"Hannah," I said, tortured.

"What is this pull between us?" she whispered again, her words frantic and fast. "I cannot seem to escape this feeling of wanting to be closer. Wanting to feel you."

I groaned. "Hannah, I wanted—"

"Mr. Windham, I took the liberty of—oh, my apologies," another voice said.

My cook, whose recipes and flavor were unmatched in all ways, was suddenly very ripe for the firing. I stepped back quickly, leaving Hannah's hands hovering in the air for a long moment, her face confused and more than a little pink.

"Ms. Chavez, what were you saying?" I forced the words out, nearly painful in my need to press back up against Hannah after her confession. To tell her that she wasn't alone at all. That she was everything I could imagine wanting. And more.

"I prepared a late lunch and a frozen dinner for this weekend." Ms. Chavez looked properly embarrassed as she gestured back over her shoulder towards the kitchen.

"Thank you, Ms. Chavez. That will be all."

"Goodbye, Mr. Windham. I will see you soon." Ms. Chavez waved and disappeared around a corner, leaving Hannah and me alone once more.

I cleared my throat. "I'm sorry for the interruption."

"Not at all. I'd love to have some lunch while I settle in. And it's almost time for you to meet with the board, isn't it?" Hannah looked everywhere but at me, her knuckles white as she intertwined her fingers.

The moment was gone. I sighed, pushing a polite smile to my lips. "Of course. I'll show you where you can settle in."

***

Chapter 5

Hannah

"Mother, I've told you a hundred times. It's not going to happen." I slapped a long piece of tape across the top of the box in front of me.

"You are so young, Hannah. You don't know what you are getting into."

"I believe you've mentioned it."

"A baby should have their father. Brandon wants to be that father."

"No, he doesn't. He hasn't wanted anything to do with me since the day I took the test." I pinned her with my best glare. She didn't budge from the doorway to my bedroom, where she'd been supervising my packing. "Do you think I've not thought this through? Kristin said I can crash with her until my new place is ready. Now that I have my job, everything will smooth out. You'll see."

She mumbled something negative sounding that I chose to ignore.

I stood, my legs completely numb from my awkward position on the floor.

"I cannot believe my first grandchild will be born like this, out of wedlock and into chaos."

"Well, I can't believe you're throwing me out only a few weeks after I came to you for help and advice."

"We need the room."

I snorted. There was no way that either of my parents needed this room. I glanced around the soft-pink walls, still decorated with posters from my youth. Tears pricked at the backs of my eyes, but I refuse to let them fall. I did not want my mother to know how much it had hurt. First Brandon's blatant rejection of both the baby and me. And now my parents'.

I swallowed the pain, my fingers digging into the box in front of me.

"I'll be gone by tomorrow. Then the room will be whatever you want it to be. I hope that it doesn't disappoint you as much as I did."

I wondered briefly if the break in my heart was audible, but she didn't respond. A second later, I heard her footsteps departing down the hall of my childhood home.

**

Declan

It was late. Too late to call.

But at the same time. She was my assistant now, and in all honesty, I needed to get her a list of things to do before I left for my last-minute flight tomorrow.

My thumb hovered over the phone, hesitating one last second.

"Grow some balls, Windham," I cursed myself, stamping my finger down on the small icon that read *Hannah Palazzo*.

A moment later, barely before the phone had time to ring through, her voice answered.

"'Ello?"

There was something wrong. Her voice was thick and deep. "Hannah?"

"Yes, hello, sir. Sorry. Frog in my throat."

I gripped my briefcase hard. "Hannah, don't lie to me."

"It's nothing, Declan. Did you need something, sir?"

"Tell me what's going on first."

"I'm uh…moving out today. It was harder than I expected."

My chest ached, picturing her homeless, holding her boxes all alone. My feet were moving before the words left my mouth. "Where are you?"

"What?"

"Hannah Palazzo, tell me where you are. Now."

"Storage place off of Vista and 18th."

"Don't go anywhere. I'm on my way."

There was silence echoing through the phone and louder than any words she could've spoken. When she spoke again, her voice was ragged. I could feel the tears there, and I broke into a jog, grateful for the fact that I'd driven myself today.

"Okay" was all she said.

I hung up as I reached the car, threw my briefcase into the back seat, and then put the Audi into gear.

I had somewhere to be.

The city passed in a blur, and as I turned into the dingy little storage facility, I saw her instantly, her petite figure leaning against her sedan. The oddest urge to tell her to stay inside, to lock her doors and be safe, rose in my throat. I stomped it down, reminding myself she'd had a shit day and there was no way she wanted safety advice from her boss.

But when my feet hit the cement, there was nothing that could stop me from jogging over to her. One hand fell to her shoulder. The other I tucked under her chin and forced her to look up at me. Shining blue eyes, rimmed in red, met mine. Misery swam in those depths, and it horrified me.

Hannah Palazzo should never hurt like this. And I wanted to do everything in my power to make sure she never did again.

"What do you need?"

Hannah blinked hard. "I don't know. I'm not sure why you are here."

"Because you shouldn't be moving alone. It's dangerous."

For a moment her eyes bugged out, even more panic filling her face. "What?"

"It's dark. This area isn't great. I wasn't about to let you be here alone, especially when I know you've been crying."

A tear broke free, slipping down her cheek as she sniffled. I brushed it away with a thumb, pushing down the urge to press a kiss there too, to chase away those sad thoughts.

"Thank you, Declan," she murmured. "I didn't think…"

"Just promise me that next time you'll call."

Her pretty lips parted, a sharp breath drawing across her lips. "I've never had anybody I could call before."

I groaned, my forehead dropping to press against her hairline. "I will always come for you. You should know that."

She pressed into me ever so slightly. "I'll remember."

Emotion rose between us, thick and hot and tempting. It would be so easy to slip a hand down her sides, to fill my hands with those smooth curves. To kiss her until she forgot all about her pain. And hold her until I was sure that she was safe.

It was my job to protect her.

Fuck.

She needed this job.

And I was a beast, leaning over her beautiful face and threatening to ruin it all for her.

I forced myself to take one, then another, step back from her. Hannah raised her hands to press against her cheeks, looking at me with more than a little confusion in her eyes.

"Okay, which one is yours?"

She pointed shyly at the half-open door a few yards ahead. Grinning, I helped myself to the first box I saw.

***

Chapter 6

Hannah

My evening was taking a drastic turn, and for the first time in a long time, I was happy to just go with it. One moment I was crying, choking back tears as I sat outside my depressing little storage unit. The next moment, Declan was storming the parking lot, his face full of worry.

He'd held me cradled against his chest, and I'd realized just how much stress I'd been carrying around. The words from my mother had suddenly faded, replaced by the way he'd made me promise to call him.

And now I was sitting across from him in an all-night diner. With his dress shirt unbuttoned and his suit jacket thrown to the side, he looked more relatable than I'd ever seen him. But there was something there still, that cool, powerful control that simmered under the surface.

Declan picked up the cheap coffee mug, his hands dwarfing it as he lifted it to relaxed lips. I shifted on the bench, my belly clenching with need as I thought back to those hands on me.

I shook my head, picking up a menu.

"Thinking of changing your mind?"

"No, I'm happy about my pancakes. I just..." I trailed off. "I feel like I have to do something with my hands."

Declan's brows rose, and something resembling a smirk pulled at his mouth. He took another sip. "I just handled all your personal belongings. Yet I still make you nervous?"

My cheeks were burning hot. "Yes, somewhat. I mean, have you seen yourself? You're…well…you. And I'm just me."

"Just you? I'm not sure I understand."

I shifted back as the waitress interrupted us to place a Reuben sandwich in front of Declan and a short stack of pancakes in front of me.

"I'm an almost graduated, barely making it assistant who just called her boss crying."

Declan's hand snapped across the table to press against my arm. His face was surprisingly angry. "First, I called you. Secondly, you, Hannah Palazzo, are amazing. I never want to hear you talking about yourself like that. And finally, you're my assistant, which makes you the best in the city."

Hysteria bubbled up in my chest, and at his last line I burst out laughing. "Amazing? You're rather full of yourself tonight."

"Moving stuff brings out the smart-ass in me."

"Note to self," I said, my giggles finally dying out. Swirling a fork, I stabbed into my pancakes. They exploded in my mouth with buttery perfection. "Oh my God, these are heaven." I moaned as I shoveled another bite in.

I swallowed, raising my eyes to find Declan staring at me, his eyes dark and serious once again. His dimple was gone. In its place was rampant hunger.

I recognized it because I felt it too, unfurling in my chest. With only the table between us, I didn't stop myself from letting the edge of my sandals brush up against his ankle.

Declan didn't move a muscle, but I could see the change in his face and the pulse of the vein across his temple.

My heart raced, and heat flooded through my body, centering on that little touch.

"Amazing," he echoed suddenly. His gaze swept over my face. "Someday I'll prove it to you."

I swallowed. "I hope you do."

I was in so far over my head.

And had no interest in changing that anytime soon.

***

I'd been Declan Windham's assistant for almost a month, and somehow, I'd managed to keep both my own desires and what I was guessing was his in check. After the close call at his house, Declan had seemed to withdraw, hiding in his office for long stints in time. But even then, the few times we were alone, we ended up close.

I told him about my dream to be the first in my family to graduate from college. He told me hadn't been to a beach since he was a child. Our conversation was easy. Comfortable. And I suddenly found myself craving more of that attention.

And then things stopped. Sharp as a blade to the heart, our interactions were cut off. At first, he was simply overscheduled. Busy. It made sense. But more recently, Declan wasn't coming into the office at all.

At first I'd worried that perhaps I was reading too far into the situation. But soon, his partners, Mr. Calvin and Mr. Rayne, had come to me, asking me if everything was okay with him. Still, Declan continued to cancel meeting after meeting, claiming he needed to work from his home office and was simply too busy to come in.

And while I appreciated the distance in a professional sense, I wouldn't lie—I missed Declan's presence, his easy authority and affection, and the way he had taken care of me. In the weeks following our first visit to his house, I found myself watching my phone, staring at our text chain and hoping that he might request me to drive out. But nothing came.

The logical part of my mind savored this freedom. I'd been able to dive into my daily tasks. I'd made friends with some of my coworkers and even gotten to my appointments without anyone knowing any different. And while my confidence in my job soared, my once tiny bump continued to grow.

This morning getting dressed had been an entire production, and the zipper on my skirt was straining against my skin. I knew my days were limited until someone noticed. But for now, I would keep my head down and attempt to be as invaluable to Declan as I possibly could. Even if I had to do it at a distance.

Taking a deep breath, I focused on the files in front of me, sorting and filing. Sorting and filing. Over and over until I had to push away to take a break, pressing a hand against the growing bump in my abdomen. I hadn't had much morning sickness, but today I was feeling quite nauseated.

I sent a prayer heavenward that Declan wouldn't need much done today. I was in rough shape and by lunch was considering how unprofessional it might be to go take a nap on Declan's office sofa.

My throat grew tight. I would have to tell him soon. My naturally lanky figure had hid the baby for longer than even I had hoped. But there would obviously be questions when I started showing up to work every day with a bump the size of a basketball.

Tears threatened. I turned away from Tyler's ever-present eyes. He had become a friend, I thought. I wasn't so sure that he wouldn't turn me in to save his skin, but the other assistants had been kind and helpful as I found my bearings here at Calvin, Windham and Rayne. And I appreciated that.

My phone suddenly buzzed across my desk, making me jump. "Hello?"

"Hannah, this is Declan. I'm working from my home office today, but I badly need one of the drives at my desk. Would you mind bringing it to me?"

I bit my lip, fighting back a groan. Today or all days. "Of course, sir. Should I call a car service?"

"Already called. You just have to get in. He's waiting down by the back gates." Declan's voice was short, and for some reason it only made my eyes water more. Stupid hormones.

I sniffled, grabbing a Kleenex to blot up the tears and running nose as I began to gather my things. "Great. I'll see you soon," I said, my legs already in motion.

***

Chapter 7

Hannah

I spent most of the hour drive there clutching the carefully packaged drive on my lap, eyes closed, trying to take deep breaths, and reminding myself that I would not, could not get sick in Declan's fancy car.

I wasn't sure if the driver could sense the urgency of getting me out of the vehicle or if traffic was kind today, but it felt like we made record time. The moment the car stopped, I threw open the door and dragged in a huge lungful of the fresh air, desperate to quiet the storm in my stomach.

"Ms. Palazzo? Are you all right?" The driver's kind voice reminded me of what I was here to do. I straightened, slowly, the ground under my feet still undulating.

I lied easily. The same lie I'd been telling everybody for weeks. "I'm fine, thank you."

"Are you going back to the city tonight?"

Just the thought of getting back onto the highway, the cars speeding and bumping and hurtling, made my stomach contents rise in my throat. I pressed a hand there, a finger raised as I pleaded with him to stop talking.

M y words come out hushed, my mind solely focused on getting into Declan's house. "I'll let you know as soon as I know."

"Do you need a hand inside, Ms. Palazzo? You're looking very pale."

"Just a little stomach bug, I'm sure," I assured him, waving him off as I stepped towards the door. One step after another, farther up the walk, until I could slip through the double doors. The whole time I promised myself that all I had to do was get Declan the information he needed and then I could go lie down for a while. Even Declan wouldn't be that cold to not let me relax.

"Mr. Windham?" I called into the entryway. Marble tiles swam in my vision, and I braced my hand against the wall. After a moment, I pushed my forehead there too, desperate to anchor myself to something solid, to stop the horrible lurching in my stomach.

"Please, baby, not now," I whispered desperately. My eyes flooded with anguished tears. "Mr. Windham? Declan?" I raised my voice again, too afraid to move from my position.

"Hannah? What's going on? Christ! What's wrong?" Those familiar hands were suddenly against my back, sliding across my shoulders as he pulled my bag from my hands. I distinctly heard the drive crash to the floor. I wanted to protest, but the words never came.

"So dizzy," I finally murmured, pressing a hand against my belly as if the baby inside had any control of what they were doing to my body.

"Fuck, Hannah. Can you walk?" He'd lost that cold tone, his words tainted with worry as I felt the coolness of his fingers press against my neck and face.

I shook my head frantically. "I can't. I'll get sick on your beautiful floors."

"Fuck the floors," I heard him mutter. Then I heard a small grunt felt my feet become airborne, my body tucked against the hard, muscled lines of his chest. With a groan, I tucked myself closer, trading the wall for his neck as I sought out this minute pleasure, this release from the sickness that gripped me so tightly.

"Easy, sweetheart. Easy. I've got you." We were moving, his stockinged feet making almost no noise as we moved through the house. I clamped my eyes shut, huffing in the scent of him as I waited, terrified of what might be next.

Softness, smelling like lavender and cucumber, was what I felt next. My face settled against a pillow, and I could feel satin-like sheets slipping over my bare legs as his hands smoothed over my suit jacket, unbuttoning the trio of shining buttons and tearing it from my shoulders.

Next was my skirt. I could feel his fingers hesitate there before the zipper lowered, releasing a bit more of my belly. My eyes flew open. Belly. Oh my God, he was going to see everything. I wriggled on the blankets, trying to reach around, to stop him, to get ahead of him.

"Easy. It's me. I'm not taking it off, just trying to make you comfortable," he said calmly, his hands steady on my hip and leg. He clearly didn't understand why I was panicking.

"Wait, please." I pressed my hands against my front. He must have already unsnapped it, as the fabric loosened, sending a welcome relief through my system.

Suddenly the belly pain lessened. And while my dizziness pushed on. I could finally put more than two words together. "I'm okay. Just need a moment."

"Don't you dare say that. I'm the one who just carried you up here. Something is wrong, Hannah. I'm calling the doctor."

"No! No, please!" I begged, my hands reaching out and finding him. I held on to his fingers with every ounce of strength I had left.

I could hear the pain in his voice. "I can't let you be like this. I have to get you help." After a long moment, he pulled from of my hands and began to stroke my back in long, gentle pulses.

I sniffled, the emotions of the day roaring through my system. "There's nothing you can do. It's morning sickness."

"Morning sickness?"

"Yes, morning sickness. I'm pregnant."

The pain was lessening again as his hands continued their gentle rubbing across my shoulders. But his voice was flat when he asked, "Where's the father? I should call him and let him know you're sick."

I pressed my face into the pillow, my secrets burning as they broke free. "No father. He doesn't want us. Please, just let me take a break. I'll be ready to get up in just a minute. The drive. I brought you it."

"Shh." His hands smoothed the hair on my brow. And against all my reservations, I pressed up, begging for more of that quiet attention. "I'm here."

I curled my fingers into the softness of the pillow and closed my eyes as I gave into the moment and let the darkness sweep over me.

***

Declan
Pregnant.

Hannah was pregnant.

Suddenly the tiny little observations, the confusion over her reactions, made more sense.

And stupid me, who had been working her to all hours of the night, trying to drown myself and her in a mountain or work. Enough that it would keep me from making a move that she clearly didn't want.

But not today. Today she had clutched on to me, her fingernails digging in as she poured out her secret and pain. I could feel her anguish. And I almost wished she'd wake up so I could tell her how little that meant to me. If anything, it made me want her even more.

Her words still echoed in my ears. "No father," she had said. "He doesn't want us."

Fuck that guy. I wanted both of them. In her sleep, she'd curled against me. From my position at the edge of the bed, I could see the change of shape just above her hips. I couldn't believe she'd managed to zip herself into her skirt with a baby bump that size.

I suddenly cursed my inability to read into things. Pulling out my phone, I made a series of purchases and emails before tucking the phone back in my pocket. She would not have to do this alone. Not anymore.

Gently, more so than I'd ever treated anything else, I let my fingers trail across the exposed strip of skin that I'd opened up in my attempts to make her more comfortable. The skin there was silken but also as firm and solid as stone. The baby inside stretching her body as he or she made themselves known. I smiled at the little bump, pressing my hand there for just a moment.

"It's going to be okay; I've got you," I said to the baby, my voice low and tight. "You're safe now."

As if sensing a change, Hannah rolled onto her back, exposing more of her smooth, pale skin. I smiled at her dozing form then quickly tucked her into bed.

It physically hurt to leave her, but I had a few things to sort out, and I thought it was better I get a start before she woke up. I wanted to be able to get her anything she might need when she woke up.

After all, her care and livelihood were my priority now.

***

Chapter 8

Hannah

The silken comfort that I found myself in was foreign and yet still familiar. I turned my nose in deep, breathing in the comforting smell. Declan. It had to be Declan's bed.

I shot up in bed, one hand flying across my belly to cup the small bump that was now freed from its prison of pencil skirt hell.

"Oh no, oh no, oh no!" I chanted, swinging my feet to the ground. Pausing, I waited to see if the morning sickness was about to overwhelm me once more.

Nothing.

Thank God. I turned, patting the fluffy covers in an effort to find my phone or laptop or anything that might connect me with the outside world. My fingers brushed against a bright green Post-It note perched atop a pile of soft-looking clothing. I read it aloud, my heart hammering.

Didn't want to wake you. There's ginger ale in the fridge under the nightstand and crackers in the drawer. Come down when you're ready.

My heart continued pounding in my chest. I read the letter again. And once more. Ginger ale and crackers? I opened the drawer slowly, eyeing the plain saltines that lay inside. My stomach remained content for the moment, so I switched to the fridge, where a trio of ginger ales stood happily waiting for me. Cracking one open, I let the spiced beverage work its magic on my stomach as I sat on the edge of the bed, sipping slowly.

I did feel much better. Guilt swept through me, and I pressed a hand to my bump. This week has been rougher than I figured. I'd hoped the apartment I wanted would be open soon, but as of now, I was stuck couch-surfing for the next two weeks, and obviously it didn't agree with me.

I cringed just thinking of going back to my friend Kristen's house tonight. She was a great friend, but between her, her roommates, and the lack of space, it was more than crowded there. And it seemed like as soon as I got behind on rest, the baby would quickly remind me that I needed to be taking it easy.

"I'm sorry, little one," I murmured, pressing against that firm bump as I stood, carrying my ginger ale. "We should probably go face the music, shouldn't we? No one wants an unwed mother who doesn't even have her degree."

My skirt completely refused to zip up again, so I tugged on the fleece-lined sweatpants and put my arms through the hoodie. They were huge on me, but my body sagged in relief as I was able to swap out my too-tight clothes. I sniffed back the tears that lurked at the edges of my eyes as I opened the bedroom door and peeked out into the hall.

No Declan. The wave of disappointment that flowed over me was nothing new. I'd felt that every day that I didn't have a chance to spend my days alongside the charismatic man. And now he'd seen me at my absolute worst. And still left me a sweet note and snacks to calm my stomach.

I didn't deserve him. Even if I wanted him.

Padding in my bare feet down the hall, I followed the sounds of TV and made my way down to the living portion of the house. It had gotten dark outside, and I wondered briefly how long I'd been asleep.

"Declan?" I called out softly. I could hear the TV from the living room, see the colorful lights dancing against the wall as I moved closer.

"Hannah!" His voice was surprised as he spotted me hovering in the back of the room. He stood quickly, setting his laptop aside. "You should've called. How are you feeling?"

"Better, I think." I held up the ginger ale. Then I felt the oncoming tears. He must've too because I felt him hurry to meet me. "Also, so embarrassed." The last word was punctuated with a soft sob as my shoulders gave way, my chin dropping as I sagged into his body. "So embarrassed."

"Embarrassed? Oh sweetheart, no." His arms were around me, cradling me close as I pressed my face against his shoulder. The softness of his cotton tee comforted me as my body finally gave into the stresses of the last few weeks.

He ran his hands slowly up and down my spine, his body wrapped around me as he held me tightly, not letting me go until the sobs finally quieted and slowed.

"And now I just cried all over you."

He looked me dead in the eye. "But you didn't throw up on the floors."

I snorted out a laugh, looking around in a fruitless attempt to find something to wipe my leaking eyes and nose on. "Ha, ha," I said sarcastically.

He smiled at me, those perfect lips bowed. "Just trying to make you feel better."

"You've done more than anyone else," I admitted as he drew me into the living room and onto a wide sectional sofa.

Hitting mute on the sports channel, he settled us both down into the cushions.

"I'm sure you must have a hundred questions."

He watched me closely. "Not a hundred, and none until you are ready to talk about them."

"What? You're my boss. Surely I owe you some kind of explanation."

"You're a beautiful young woman who happens to be pregnant. You owe me no explanation."

I could feel my gaze darting around the room, suddenly unsure of myself once more. Because in some way I'd hoped that my confession would finally allow me to talk about the elephant in the room. Or, in this case, the baby in my belly.

"I'm staying with friends while my apartment is prepared. I've not been sleeping well, and somehow that makes my morning sickness much, much worse. I'm sorry. I should've warned you or sent Tyler instead of collapsing in your house."

"You didn't need to do anything else. You did your best. It's not your fault that you're tired."

"But it is. Because I'm the one who got pregnant and ruined everything."

To my surprise, Declan's face darkened. "Did he tell you that? The father."

I bit my lip. "Yes. Him. And after he left, my parents did too. They told me I let them down. They asked me to move out. Immediately."

Declan's face contorted, the vein in his forehead pulsing as he ran his thumb over the top of my knuckles. "I'm so sorry he talked to you like that. Family, babies most of all, are supposed to be cherished. I don't see anything ruined, certainly nothing tarnished."

His gaze held mine, intense and vulnerable.

"I was an accidental child. I spent my youth being moved from foster family to foster family until I was old enough to get myself to school on time. You grow up fast when you live in a household that reminds you constantly of how little you were wanted. And later how little you would amount to."

My hand covered my face, the ache in my chest incredible. Declan's family had done that. How could anybody not want him? An image of a younger Declan, gangly and dimple-cheeked, surged through my mind. Hurt and anger swirled in my belly on his behalf.

"They were wrong though. Look at you! You made your life into something great."

Declan's chest rose and fell. "You really believe that, don't you?"

"Of course I do. I wouldn't lie. Not even to you."

"I've discovered that even in my successes, I've forgotten one very valuable part of my life. One that I suddenly find myself convinced I should fix." His hand reached between us, fingers tucking a rogue strand of my hair away from my face.

My heart pounded in my ears.

"I've never been able to find someone to share my success with. My life. It leaves me feeling empty most nights. At least until lately."

I couldn't stop myself from asking, "What changed?"

Declan leaned into me, his forehead coming to rest against mine. "I met someone. Someone kind. Someone beautiful. Someone who makes me want to believe in family dinners and trips to the beach."

My eyes fluttered shut. Disbelief and excitement hummed through my body. "Declan…"

"Hannah?" It was a question. A request.

I nodded eagerly, and a moment later I could taste the sweetness of Declan's lips as he leaned in to kiss me.

The touch of his skin on mine made my blood rush. Energy suddenly coursed through my body, and I dug my hands into the silken strands of his hair.

More. I needed more. But he was pulling away, offering soft words, tiny little kisses up my jaw as he pulled me tightly to his body on the couch.

I whimpered but allowed it. As he drew me in, it made me wish I could curl up in his lap and let him hold me until I had forgotten all those horrible words.

My hand had stolen around my bump again. "In case there was ever confusion, I do want this baby. They will be so loved. I will make sure of it, even if I do it alone." I sounded far braver than I truly was.

"I didn't doubt it for a minute."

We sat in comfortable silence, his lips content to press against my temple. And impossibly, my eyes began to droop. "Would it be okay if I sat here with you? Just a little while before I head home?"

"Home? I thought your parents kicked you out?"

I cringed. Oh yes, of course, I didn't have a home anymore. "Back to where I'm staying, then. Kristen's place."

"That's what I wanted to talk to you about." Declan shifted on the couch, his arm brushing mine. "I'd like to offer you a place to stay. Somewhere safe for you and your baby."

His hand reached out, hesitating only a moment before pressing against my belly. My heart thundered in my chest. "I can't sleep at night not knowing you're safe. I won't bother you. I will stay at the apartment, or if you'd rather be there, I will stay here. I just need to be sure you're safe."

"Why?" Something low in my belly quivered, hope making my breath come short in my lungs.

"Because you're special and you deserve to know that. I will do absolutely anything to prove to you that you deserve the world."

Tingles broke out over my body, making me shiver as I processed his words. Was he saying what I thought he was? Emboldened by that kiss, I pushed on. Suddenly I needed to know, more than anything else, if I was the only one feeling this pull between us.

"What about you, Declan?"

"Me?"

"What do you deserve? Have you been hiding here?"

I felt more than saw his broad shoulders shift in the cushions. He was uncomfortable. "We aren't talking about me." Any other day, I might've backed down. But not tonight.

"We should. You're here, taking care of me, protecting me, holding me as I cry all over you. Never asking for what you really want. I need to know."

His eyes blazed. "Because I'm afraid to ask for what I want. It was safer to stay away."

"Don't stay away, please." I moved closer, my fingers seeking out his flesh. I found his thigh first, slipping over his knee, feeling the softness of his sweatpants and the firmness of the muscle just within. The bright memory of his kisses burns in my mind. "Tell me."

For a moment, Declan seemed to hold back, his entire body tense on the couch. And then he snapped, his hands slipping around my waist to haul me over his lap, my legs sitting on either side of his hips.

My hair slipped around us like a strawberry curtain, and my breathing hitched. His hands were stroking down my back, soft and careful.

"Tell me," I pushed him again, unafraid, and powerful. It felt like the first time I'd been in control of my life in months.

Declan pulled me forward, my crotch settling over the hard length of him, making both of us gasp with pleasure. "I want you, Hannah. I've wanted you since the moment I met you."

Declan leaned in, his lips finding the pulse at my neck and pressing a gentle kiss there. I groaned, my hips jerking at the pleasure rocketing through me.

"You want me," I echoed, my hands finding purchase on the powerful line of his shoulders.

"More than anything else in the entire fucking world. And not just this body." His hands trailed up and down my sides. "All of you."

"But..." I hesitated, almost pulling away as my body quickly reminded me of the reason I was at this man's house at all. The baby between us. Declan took my hesitation for opportunity and began to press more kisses down my neck, the hot slide of his tongue teasing every line and vein there as he made his way towards my chest. "The baby?"

He growled there, the gentle vibrations making my belly tighten with need. "I want all of you. *Both* of you." To emphasize his point, Declan dropped a hand to press over the baby, his breathing hitching.

"I've been waiting for a family of my own my entire adult life. This baby is yours, which makes them mine too. If you let me claim you both, I would. Happily, for every day of the rest of my life."

"Oh God," I said, my head tilting back as I pressed a hand over the top of his. "Do you mean that?"

"Every word. And I hope that you let me take care of you, let me love you how you deserve. And that we fill up this enormous fucking house with gorgeous babies that have your eyes and my last name."

"Declan," I murmured. "Yes, yes. That's all I want."

"Tell me, then. Tell me I can have you."

"I'm already yours."

***

Chapter 9

Declan

I must've hallucinated. Because if I wasn't, then my literal dream woman had just told me she was mine for the taking.

I choked back the wave of need that threatened to break loose at any moment. All it would take was permission from those perfect lips, or God help me, another movement from those blessed hips that she still held over my cock.

"I won't rush you, Hannah. Take as long as you need." I could wait for her.

"My parents threw me out. My ex-boyfriend turned out to be a total fake. You and this baby, you're the only good things in my life right now." She leaned in, pressing her forehead against mine and grinding gently against me once again.

I groaned, my balls tight. For a moment, I was afraid I'd lose control completely, come in my pants before I even got inside her.

"I don't want to wait any longer. Because I've wanted you too. I've had this need, this impulse to get myself as close to you as possible. Ever since my interview. You're good, you're kind, and I can feel every move you make. I wanted to tell you, but I was so scared. A man like you with me?" Her lips quivered.

"Stop that now. We found a way to each other, right? Maybe we have the baby to thank for that."

She chuckled, the sound a little wet as her tears slowed. I brushed away a last tear, slipping my hand down the softness of her cheek to hold her there.

"You'll stay here, then?"

"That's too much…"

I shushed her, pressing a finger over her lips, silencing her.

A soft, slow smile pulled at her lips. Not moving my hand away, she reached around to grip my wrist and nodded. "I'll stay," she said against the pad of my finger. Close enough that her tongue clipped my flesh as she spoke.

"I should get you settled, comfortable. You need your rest."

"I'm quite comfortable where I am." Her words were barely audible, but the heat in her eyes was clear to both me *and* my cock. Her lips parted, and impossibly bold, she swiped her tongue over my digit.

"Fuck, Hannah, you don't know what you're saying."

"I know exactly what I'm saying." She shifted closer. "Please, Declan, take care of me. I need it."

Her hands were tight on my shoulders, her fingernails sharp and persistent.

I moved my hand to her face, turning it to mine, holding her tight to me. "Say it again, now."

She was panting. "I want you."

"Thank God." I barely got the words out before I captured her lips. I attempted to be gentle. I wanted to wait, to let her come to me, but the minute her lips found mine, I felt her sag against me. Her hands gripped my shoulders, but they were loose, almost unsure of what to do with me.

But her lips, that was what made me lose control. The sweetness of her surrender as she parted her lips and let me in. The first taste of the honey there, it was the beginning of addiction. One that I didn't feel guilty for. One I wouldn't be able to resist.

And I didn't. I kissed her again and again. Tangling my tongue with the slick honey of hers, capturing the noises that she made in the back of her throat as we writhed together on the couch. Her borrowed shirt was riding up her belly now, and I could feel the heat of her, hovering over my hardness.

I let my hands find her thighs, slipping under her waistband to rub my thumbs across the soft flesh there, before I delved in, filling my hands with the perfect globes of her ass.

"Fuck, sweetheart, you're perfection."

I dared to slip a finger low, teasing the edge of her lips. With a soft gasp, she arched her back, letting my finger sink into her heat.

"Oh God, Hannah, you're drenched."

She pressed soft, open-mouthed kisses down my neck. "I've been waiting a month for you to touch me. You can't blame me."

"I don't, but we've got to go slow. I don't want to hurt you." I retreated, pressing a hand against her belly again. Hazy eyes met mine as she quirked her lips in a soft smile.

"The only thing that's hurting me now is not being able to be with you. Don't stop, Declan, not now."

I could barely register her words before her hand slipped between us and brushing straight by mine. She ran fingers over the bulge in my sweatpants. An instant later, wide blue eyes found mine. "Wow."

I chuckled, pulling her hand away with a dejected sigh. "As good as that is for my ego, I can't let you down there yet."

"Why? I want to."

"Because I want to be inside you when I come."

Her cheeks went bright pink. "Oh, my. I..." she stuttered a little, tucking her hand back around my neck.

"Tell me what kind of experience you've had."

"Just the one boyfriend. We weren't—" she hesitated, teeth teasing at her bottom lip "—compatible. So, after the first few times, he wasn't all that interested anymore. Then after the baby, he was out of the picture completely."

"Compatible?"

She looked down. "He said it was my fault, that I couldn't get 'there'...for him."

I stared at her as realization took hold. "He never made you come. Ever?"

"It was only a few times. But, no, I couldn't." She tightened her hold on me. "Don't worry though. I enjoy giving pleasure too."

I surged to my feet, my temples throbbing as the blood rushed to my head. Hannah squealed, her legs snapping around my waist as she attempted to hold on to me. "What are you doing? Declan?"

"We're going upstairs."

"Did I say something wrong?"

"Never. I'm about to right a wrong," I said, my teeth gritted. I couldn't believe what I'd just heard. Not only was that horrible man responsible for abandoning Hannah and her baby, but he'd apparently completely ruined Hannah's way of thinking about sex.

I was going to fix that. Now.

I strode into my room, setting Hannah down on the edge of the bed. Her face was still confused, but I could see the heat in her eyes as I stepped back and stripped off my T-shirt. Her lips parted as her chest rose and fell quickly.

"Can I touch you?" she asked, almost too soft to hear.

"I'm yours." I dropped down beside her, bracing myself for the perfect torture of her skin on mine. Her fingers were tentative, just barely skimming my flesh as she moved her hands over my chest, my shoulders, down to the springy dark curls that covered my belly and disappeared into my sweatpants.

"You're gorgeous," she said, awed.

My cock, already standing tall and needy, ached even further. I took great care in my appearance, and having this woman admire me only further emphasized how great we would be together.

As soon as I made sure she understood pleasure. I wanted to teach her, to let her feel what it could be like. And then I would show her how it could be like with me. The anticipation might kill me, but the rewards would be endless.

"Thank you. I could say the same thing." I rose up over her, urging her to lie back as I hovered over her. With a few quick tugs, I had those sweatpants down her legs and my borrowed shirt was hurled to a corner. I was rewarded with my efforts by the perfect, creamy expanse of skin. Surprisingly, her clothing had hidden a sprinkling of freckles. I made a vow then and there to chart each of them as if they were stars in the sky. She would be the moon, and I would worship her.

"Declan…" She fidgeted under me.

"Let me love you, sweetheart. You just tell me what you do or don't like. Alright?"

Wordlessly she nodded, settling her shoulder back into the softness of my bedcovers. I leaned over her, pressing a kiss, then two, as I moved up her leg, tracing the lines of her lean frame, the long muscles that flexed and relaxed under my lips.

"Still okay?" I asked, switching to the other leg, pressing her knee up and back as my eyes zeroed in on the core of her.

She mumbled something, and I let my gaze slide up, confirming that she was enjoying it. The sight awaiting me was almost enough to make me come right there. Her body, soft and curving, was arched skyward. Her hands were fisted in the blankets, and her eyes were closed tight. Her belly was rounded and looked soft and feminine, and my mouth watered as I watched her savor her pleasure.

The pleasure I was giving her.

I knew then and there: I would gladly spend every waking moment of my life making her feel exactly like this. She would only know me like this. Ever.

"Yes, Declan, touch me."

Her wish was my command. But my control was quickly fraying. I was only human after all. I pressed my lips to the apex of her thigh, the lace of her panties rough against my lips. Her intake of breath was my final trigger. I darted my tongue out, seeking more of those sounds, more of the sweetness from her.

I pulled away just enough to tug her panties down, over her knees and onto the ground, exposing the perfect pink flesh to my eyes. I groaned, settling back down between her legs, which she parted eagerly.

This time when my breath warmed the most private part of her, her hips rose, begging and needy to my mouth. I hummed in gratitude, pressing a simple, warm kiss against her. Rewarding her pursuit of pleasure with more, I let my tongue slip out to taste her.

The noise she made was something between a squeal of surprise and a plea for more. I took it as encouragement and did it again. My tongue darted over her again and again, urging her to participate, to rise up against my kisses.

"Good girl," I said against her skin, my hands finding her thighs and opening her wider. "Now, let me taste you."

There was no more teasing left in me. I wanted to hear her scream. I wanted to feel the honey of her release coat my tongue. I wanted it more than my next breath, which should've been obvious as I buried my face completely into the musky perfection of her lips.

And I let my tongue, my mouth do the work, sucking and playing, teasing and tasting. Her delicious little sounds drove me on and on, until I could feel the quiver and pulse under my tongue. She was close. I could feel it.

Rising up on an elbow, I let my eyes drink her in once more, my cock steel as I press it into the bed. "Come for me, sweet girl," I told her, slipping a finger into the slippery heat of her and pressing forward.

I was met with tightness and a shout that tumbled from her lips. I dropped my head, slipping my tongue around her clit, and I sucked once, twice, and then I felt it. The shaking, gripping release that poured over the both of us. Her legs quivered around my shoulders, and I lapped at her honey gently, easing her through the throbbing until finally, at long last, she lay quiet under me.

I slipped my fingers from her, pressing a series of soft kisses across her pelvis as I rose up over her. "Hannah?"

"I can barely think. Declan, what was that?"

I chuckled, settling lightly over her, careful to support my own weight. "That was how it should be. And how it will always be with me."

Impossibly, her hips moved on the bed under me. I felt the softness of her skin as she pressed a hand to my side. "I still feel that throb..." Her face was flushed, but her eyes met mine with questions clear in them.

I pressed a kiss against her jaw. "I'll consider that the best compliment I've ever received."

"Declan, I think I need more." She swallowed. "I want to do it again."

"What?" My body actually shook at her words.

"I want more. I want everything. Every part of you."

***

Chapter 10

Hannah

I meant it. My brain may still be humming from the onslaught of pleasure that Declan had just coaxed out of my body, but there was still that aching emptiness at the center of me. And everything in me knew that he would be the one to fill me up. To get rid of that need forever.

I couldn't go another moment without being his. I bent a knee, urging his body to settle in more firmly against the place that still twinged and tingled from his attention.

"I don't want to hurt you."

"You won't. I want to feel you inside me. To know there is nothing between us. No more secrets, no more waiting."

"Fuck, Hannah, I'm almost out of control."

"Then let me be there for you." I dug my fingers into the softness of his hair. "I'm here for you. Right here."

His hips canted forward, the velvety soft head of his cock pressing against my wetness for only a moment before he retreated. I moaned, my head falling back into the pillows. "Declan, baby, please, fill me up."

"Fuck" was the grunted reply, his voice strained. "The mouth on you, sweetheart."

"Please" was all I got out before his hand slipped between us. I froze, waiting. And then his hips slammed forward, driving every inch of his rigid cock straight into my body.

I gasped, loudly, my body bowing up to his as I reeled in the pleasure of him. "Oh God, Declan..." My nails dug into his neck, dragging him forward and over me as he began to retreat. Then with a groan that sent fire through my blood, he thrust forward, filling me up once more.

"Hannah, Jesus, you're so tight." He drove forward again and again, the slick slide of his cock through my lips and into my body making my brain short-circuit as I began to feel that now familiar tightness bloom in my belly. Every time he stroked inside, I felt it more and more, until I could barely think straight and I was a wriggling, begging monster who needed his cock inside me like nothing ever before.

Shock warred with pleasure in my mind. I was never this girl. And with Brandon, my ex-boyfriend, it had been exciting, thrilling even, but nothing like this. Sex with Declan was a revelation.

If this was heaven, then it was also the sweetest form of death I'd ever known. And even though I knew it wasn't normal, I could feel my body gearing up to come again, encouraged by that perfect cock that settled deep and hard in my pussy every other breath.

Or maybe it had more to do with the gorgeous specimen who was pumping into me. His handsome face tensed as he drove himself home, the muscles in his arm stark as he held himself over me.

He had shown me more pleasure in this one day than I'd ever felt from any man. The comfort, the affection, and the consuming need. I wanted to return the favor.

I wrapped my legs around his waist, giving into the instincts that drove me to wrap him up, to tie him to me in the most visceral way possible. The position opened me up even wider, and I felt his sharp exhale against my shoulder.

His mouth brushed my ear, pressing hot kisses against my neck. "You're so tight, sucking me into this hot body. I need to fill you up, sweetheart."

Everything in my body clenched, desperate to experience exactly that. "Oh yes, please."

Declan's hands gripped my hips, tilting me up as he surged forward, his flesh slapping mine as he seated himself completely inside me. Then, with a flick of his thumb, he shoved me off the precipice.

With a shuddering cry, I came, my hands gripping his forearms as my body shook around him. The pleasure was undeniable, but it was nothing compared to the power that washed over me as the man above me threw back his head, the veins in his neck pronounced, a deep growl bursting from his lips as his hips rocked against mine.

I knew without asking that he was soaking me, coating me in everything that he was. The heat speared me again, setting off another wave of pleasure. I rode it, my legs still clamped, holding him desperately against me.

When his body finally ceased the shuddering movements, I felt his hands on my thighs, stoking, petting, gently easing them open.

"I don't want you to go," I admitted quietly, my heartbeat still racing.

"I'm not going anywhere. Hell, I'd live inside you if I could. I'm just switching us around so I can hold you."

Relief was a cool blanket that slipped over my shoulders. I released him enough that Declan could roll sideways, tucking me close as he settled on his back, me over the top of him.

I snuggled close, feeling more exposed than before. Declan stroked my back, the pound of his heart under my cheek lulling me into a blissful sleep.

***

Declan

She was mine.

This beautiful, sweet, delicious woman, she was mine. If I hadn't believed it before, there was no other logical answer. Not when we fit together like two puzzle pieces, her warmth the one thing capable of thawing my heart and my protection the one thing she needed the most.

Her and her baby.

No, fuck that.

My baby. I didn't care who the father was. I would be the only father this child ever knew.

I shifted my body, settling her on her side so that she wasn't pressing the firm belly of the baby between us. She mumbled then snuggled close again, tucking her nose into my neck as I resumed stroking the satin skin of her back.

While she was sleeping, I took a minute to fully appreciate the beauty of the woman I'd claimed as mine. She was a petite little thing. Her penchant for high heels disguised her stature in the office. In bed, I felt like a hulking beast next to her, which was fitting, as she stirred every primal instinct I had in me.

The perfect heart-shaped face, a long, slender neck. I looked farther, my cock stirring briefly as I watched her breasts rise and fall. She'd been sensitive there, from the pregnancy no doubt. I couldn't wait to see if they got more full, more sensitive as the baby grew. And then, after the baby, they would be full of milk for our child.

I wondered if she would still let me taste her, lick those sweet pink nipples until she dripped for me, in more ways than one.

I shuddered, my cock already hard once again, pressing tightly against the wetness of her core. I frowned, reaching between us and letting the pads of my fingers settle there. My seed was leaking from the heat of her, making her clit slick and wet.

Gently, afraid to wake her, I smeared more of my cum over her. The drive to cover every part of her was strong, and I knew that someday I would like to have her on her knees, where I could come all over that tight, gorgeous little body. Let my hands rub into her skin until there was no question who she had chosen.

I smiled, and Hannah stirred against me. I temporarily gave up my quest to cover her in my essence as I let my hand move up to rest against the firm flesh over our child.

"You're mine too," I said softly, my knuckles dancing across the skin there.

"Declan? Are you sure?"

"I've never been more sure of anything. You are meant to be mine. This child will be mine." I leaned over her, pressing a soft kiss against her nipple. Hearing her sigh, I let my tongue sweep out to tease the pink tips. "You are my priority. Just like any other baby I fill you with, my family will be the center of my everything."

I rolled her over the top of me again so I could run my thumbs over her nipples.

"You want more kids?" she whispered, her eyes half-closed.

"Yes. As many as you want to give me."

"I always wanted a big family." Her eyes closed and she leaned back, her ass settling just in front of my cock.

"I will gladly spend my days filling you with my seed—" I pressed a hand over her belly "—then watching you bloom for me."

She shuddered. "Say that again."

"Which part?" Need hit me hard. Along with pure satisfaction of the idea that this woman wanted to bear more of my children.

"Filling me with your seed."

My hands were on her hips, lifting her. Her own hands were below, seeking and finding my cock. Together, I guided her to the head. "Hannah…" Her eyes rose to mine, the pupils dark and wide. "Let me fill you up. Let me fill you with my seed, my cum, everything."

"Oh God," she cried as I arched up, sinking into that wet, quivering pussy.

"Every inch, sweetheart, every inch." I urged her to grind down, my heels pressing into the bed as she sought out the root of me.

"I can't. Help me."

With a groan, I gripped her to my chest, flipping us over. In that instant, I returned to that burning sheath my cock ached. There was no waiting this time. Her hips urgently rose to mine, accepting every driving thrust. Our ragged breaths and the slap of wet flesh were the only sounds around us.

I just stared into those beautiful blue eyes, and I drove us higher, harder, until they rolled back, her mouth falling open as her muscles clenched around me in completion.

With a ragged cry, I drove deep and held myself there, feeling the come pounding from me into her. The pleasure making my hips twitch as all thought was robbed from me.

I leaned over her, pressing my forehead to hers as we panted together. I would never be the same.

***

Chapter 11

Hannah

The past weeks had been among the best in my adult life. The days after I first gave myself to Declan were a bit of a blur, as we spent most days in bed. On the days we did leave Declan's massive bedroom, he surprised me with a variety of gifts, including a brand-new, gorgeous wardrobe of maternity clothes.

I had persisted for a long time, telling him it was too much, that it would never fit in the tiny closet of my new apartment. But then that had led straight to his next request.

He wanted me to move in with him. I still hadn't given him an answer, but I knew every day that my willpower was less and less. It was hard to resist a man like Declan Windham. Not to mention the fact that deep down, I was falling madly in love with my boss.

He treated me like a queen, true, but it was more than that. Declan valued my conversation, my opinion. His gentle authority and piercing eyes were enough to make me want to fall over myself to get to him.

With him I was cherished, adored. I rubbed a hand over the now quite noticeable bump. He wanted both of us, no doubts, no regrets.

Surprisingly, our announcement that we were together didn't shock anybody in the office. Either we were less subtle than we thought, or people were just happy to see one of the partners happily settled. For now I was continuing as his assistant, but after the baby I was planning on going back to school full time. I wanted to have that. And Declan couldn't be more supportive.

Today I was the first day I was allowed to move into my new apartment. I was going to go into town, and instead of getting the keys, I was going to fork over the fees for my cancellation. There was nowhere I wanted to be than by Declan's side. Whether that meant the office, the apartment in the city, or here, in the house we could fill with our family.

I couldn't wait to tell him. He had already driven north. A day full of meetings on the university case would keep him distracted. I grinned to myself as I climbed into my car. We'd moved it out here to one of Declan's garages when I'd begun to spend more time here outside the city.

The drive was blissfully uneventful, and by the time I arrived, I was nearly dancing in my excitement over my little idea. The apartment complex was cute. The bright verandas and big windows would've been great for the baby and me. But I didn't need that anymore.

I opened the clubhouse, looking for a landlord with whom to discuss my situation. At first, the difference from the rare sunny Chicago day into the interior left me blinded, and I blinked several times, willing my vision to clear.

But when it did, I suddenly wished I had done anything today but come here. Because standing right by one of the tall pillars was Brandon, my ex-boyfriend and the unfortunate sperm donor to the baby in my belly.

"Oh no, no, no, no," I chanted, turning and moving quickly towards the door. I cupped a hand under my belly protectively. I had to get out of here.

"Hannah! Hannah, wait!"

I didn't wait. I threw the door open wide and stumbled out onto the sidewalk. "Stay away from me, Brandon."

"I just want to talk. Five minutes." I knew he was following me. I could hear his footsteps.

"No. You've had months to talk. How did you know I'd even be here?"

"I know, I screwed up. But I called your mom. I explained what happened, our misunderstanding, so she told me where you might be. Please, love." His voice was growing more desperate.

I turned, spitting in fury. "Don't you dare call me *love*. You left us. *Left us*. There's no coming back from that. The only misunderstanding in our relationship was how I ever thought you were worth it."

Brandon, to his credit, hung his head, his shoulders low. "I know. I just wanted to see how you were."

"We," I corrected, my hand still tight around my belly. I saw his eyes focused there, but the expression on his face remained hungry, almost aggressively so. "We are doing great."

He nodded, shifting from foot to foot. "Good. I'm glad." The silence between us edged on uncomfortable as I popped a hip and glared, waiting for this to be over. It wasn't like I could outrun him in my current state. But the silence continued.

Blowing out a frustrated sigh, I turned again to leave.

"I miss you."

I opened my mouth, but he halted me by stepping closer, his hand reaching for my belly. "I missed so much."

I stepped back quickly. "Yes, you did. But the baby and I have someone else now. Someone who comes to every appointment. Who understands what I need. What we both need. He loves us."

Brandon's head snapped up, his lips thin and flat. "You're seeing someone else?"

"Yes, I am. I'm very happy with him." I wanted it to be abundantly clear that there was no coming back from this. Not with him. Not ever. Declan would be the only man in my life from here on.

To my surprise, Brandon's face went dark, angry as he jabbed a finger in my direction. "I can't believe you. You acted so innocent, pretending you were a virgin. But we both know how you begged for it. And now you've found someone else to fuck you? While my baby grows in you?"

I stared, my jaw slack. "You are out of line, Brandon. Leave us alone, or I'll call the cops." Not to mention Declan. I turned to my car, my flats slapping against the cement.

"I won't. That's my baby. No matter what he tells you, he knows it's mine."

"He wants this baby, more than you ever did." My hands shake, the key fob for my car slipping from between my fingers. I swooped down to grab it before hitting the unlock button and hurrying to climb in.

Brandon's hand snapped out, grabbing the door before I could close it. "He's lying. No man would ever want the leftovers of the guy before him. He'll leave you both. And you will come crawling back to me." He released the door, letting me slam it shut. "I'm not a patient man, Hannah, but I will wait for you."

I sped away as quickly as the Chicago traffic would allow.

***

Declan

I thought that Hannah would've been back by now. She left a text saying that she was going into town to meet up with some old friends, but I'd assumed she'd be back by now.

I palmed the small box in my jacket pocket. I'd had meetings today at the university, and while this case continued to drag on into eternity, it had given me the perfect excuse to make a trip over to my favorite jeweler and check on the status of Hannah's ring.

I'd ordered it weeks ago. I was so completely sure she was my forever. But seeing it today, so beautiful and unique, exactly like her, had set my emotions on edge. I had no doubts about the two of us and our new family. But I didn't want to rush her. She was younger than I was. She'd not experienced life like I had. And while I'd pledged to take her anywhere she liked, to support her in everything she did, there was a lingering thought in the back of my mind that I might scare her away with the force of my love and my need.

I moved into the kitchen, my phone out as I shoved the unwelcome thought from my mind and sent her a text.

Are you alright? I hope you had a good day.

Three little dots appeared; she was typing. I threw my coat aside, noting the exact location so that when I panicked about the ring missing later, I would remember where it was. My phone buzzed, and I smiled before I even unlocked the screen.

But it was a phone call. Unknown. I swiped to accept it.

"Hello, is this Hannah Palazzo?"

"I'm sorry, no. This is a…" I mulled over the identifying characteristics. "This is her boyfriend."

"Oh good. Thank you for coming by this morning. I just wanted to let you know that Ms. Palazzo still needs to come back in and sign the final documents."

"I'm sorry, who is this?"

"Stonegate Apartments? Sorry I should've said that to begin with. Would you pass along the message?"

My mind was frozen, but my blood pumped furiously through my body. What boyfriend had she been with this morning? And at her new apartment? My stupid heart ached in pain. I had been so sure of what she was going to do. That she would want to stay here with me. My fists clenched. "Sure, I'll pass it along."

I hung up quickly, striding through the house. She had to be here somewhere. "Hannah! Where are you?"

I took the stairs three at a time, my heart thundering as I hurried towards the master suite.

"Where are you?"

This time I heard it. The softest sob. I looked around the room, the empty chairs, the undisturbed bed.

"Baby?" I said softer, listening.

"I'm here. But please, don't come in."

Her voice was so quiet, I could barely make out the words. I padded through the bathroom to the master closet. I could hear the mewling cries of her voice from behind the door. I reached for the door but then waited. She had told me not to come in. Instead, I pressed an ear to the door. "Hannah, you're in the closet."

"I needed somewhere dark and quiet."

With a sigh, I bent my knees and let my back slide down the door. The tile was rock hard under my ass, but I couldn't leave her. "What happened today?"

"Brandon was waiting at the apartments. My parents told him where I'd be."

I nodded, my heart pounding. "What did he say?"

"He said he missed me." Her voice grew ever soft. "That he wanted to talk about our *misunderstanding*."

I almost shouted then, the force of my fury high in my throat. But that wouldn't do her any good. "What did you say?"

"I told him I would never forget what he did or forgive him."

I was proud of the venom in her voice. My woman was a tough little thing.

"Good girl. What else?"

"That I had someone new, who wanted me and this baby. And that he was going to take care of us." A soft sob broke the air. "He said you were lying, that no man would ever want someone else's baby."

"He's a fucking liar, Hannah. I've never..." My throat closed tight. "I've never wanted anything more than this family with you. And like I've said before, I will be there for every step of the way. All the tee-ball games, all the Halloween costumes, all the tantrums and diapers. Because I love you. And I love that baby."

The closet was silent once more.

"Do you understand?" I ran my hands over my hair. "Hold on. I'll be right back."

My heart pounding, I ran down the stairs and into the kitchen, digging out the ring box in a rush that left the cook staring. Moments later, I was back, one hand pressed against the door as I kneeled there, ring box extended and open.

"Hannah Palazzo, you are the best thing in my life. And I want to spend the rest of my life making your dreams come true. I love you, sweetheart. Will you open the door?"

The door cracked just a sliver. Then an inch. Then she was standing there, strawberry hair wild around her face. Tears making her blue eyes glow. She sniffled, her mouth a perfect *O* as she stared down at me.

"Hannah Palazzo, I want you as my wife. The mother of our children. My partner in all things." I pressed my hand to the swollen belly just at my eyeline. "Please, let me spend the rest of my life showing you how much I love you. Marry me."

Her hand clapped over her lips, eyes flooded with more tears as she looked down at me. "Yes, Declan, yes!"

With a squeal, she bowled me over, both of us tumbling back into the master bedroom as I filled my hands with the woman I loved most.

My fiancée.

My future wife.

The mother of my babies.

With a groan, I found the silky skin of her face and turned her lips to mine. I saw sparks when she kissed me back, hard and needy.

"Wait, wait. Hannah, we need to talk about this."

"Our wedding? Absolutely. But first…" Her voice trailed off as she rained kisses down my neck, over the bob of my Adam's apple.

"Fuck, sweetheart, I'm serious," I laughed, pressing her back to a sitting position. "There's something I've been thinking of for almost as long as I've been thinking about you being my wife."

"What's that?"

"Being that baby's father. I want to be sure Brandon is never able to hurt them, or you, ever again. But I need your help."

Her eyes grew round, but her hands were sure and tight against my own. "Tell me what to do."

***

Hannah

I stretched out one sandaled foot, wearily eyeing the swollen ankle as I recrossed my legs. I had always loved the summer, but this year, it was not loving me.

But maybe that was because I was well on my way to seven months pregnant and I could barely see my toes these days. Sighing, I pulled out my phone and sent Declan a text.

Hannah: My feet look like balloons.

Declan: Very cute little balloons.

Hannah: So, you say. How much longer should I wait?

Declan: Just a few minutes, then I will whisk you away for a foot massage and decaf latte.

I grinned at the phone like an idiot. My heart still fluttered at the sweet exchange. I was so distracted that I didn't see the other man who had approached me.

"Hannah?"

I jerked, my fingers slipping on the screen as I stared up at Brandon. "Brandon? I was worried you weren't coming."

"Running late from work, sorry," he grumped, sitting down opposite me and folding his hands.

"That's alright. How are you?" I bit the tip of my tongue, determined to keep my temper, and therefore Declan's, in check. With a tap on the edge of my phone, I leaned back into my chair, staring at the man I once thought would be my happily ever after.

How much more wrong could I have been?

Brandon didn't answer the question though. He eyed my belly with a strange sort of disgust. "How much longer?"

I rubbed my bump with a loving hand. "About three months. Baby is doing well."

He smiled at me crookedly. "I knew you'd call." His eyes strayed purposefully to my hand, naked and tanned.

"I wanted to give you a chance to know your child."

Brandon snorted. "The baby is fine and all, but what I want is you."

"I'm not an option, Brandon. I've told you that."

"What the hell? Are you serious?"

I turned over my hands, picking absently at the freshly done manicure. "I already told you, I found someone else."

"You're a liar, Hannah. You always were." His voice was getting louder now. And while my belly twisted with a small bout of nerves, I stayed strong.

"I'm not. I have someone very special. I wanted to give you this last opportunity."

"Well, fuck that. You and that baby mean nothing to me. You were just a quick lay and an unfortunate complication. You can lose my number. Permanently."

His face was red now, mottled and panting as he leaned over the table. More than a few patrons were staring as I picked up my ice water and took a sip.

"You're sure?"

"I'm out of here." Brandon slammed his hands on the patio table and then pushed off.

I gave the patrons a shrug and a smile and hit the record button on my phone one more time.

At roughly the same moment, Declan appeared on the sidewalk, his face thunderous as he stepped into Brandon's space. Brandon slowed, his gaze flickering over the much larger man. Declan looked down his nose at my ex-boyfriend. "You get what you need, sweetheart?"

I pushed back, standing slowly, a hand pressed to the small of my back. I held my phone up, showing the still shot of the video recording I'd just taken. "Got it."

Brandon's face went white. "What is this?"

"This is your official notice that my wife and I will be pursuing sole custody with an extensive restraining order." Declan stepped even closer, the shadow of his body slipping over Brandon like a bad omen. "That baby is mine. That woman is mine. And if you fuck with either of them, then I suggest you bring a damn good lawyer. And help. Because you'll need it to get through me."

Brandon sputtered. His shoulders hunched away from Declan's proclamation.

"Are we clear?" I said softly from behind them.

Brandon nodded, and I shook the phone at him again. "Out loud please."

"Yes, I get it. You won't see me again."

"Good," Declan said, pivoting on the sidewalk to let Brandon rush by, his feet stumbling along the path as he hurried away from us both. A wave of clapping followed me as I walked to Declan. He immediately enveloped me in his arms, the comforting strength of his muscles the thing that finally drove away the last traces of anxiety and worry over how we had to proceed with this.

"My love…" Declan pressed his hands to my back, my belly, my arms. Stroking and guiding as we moved back towards the car I knew he had waiting. "Are you okay?"

I nodded, soaking him in. "I feel good. This is what we needed to know and what I needed to do."

His fingers danced across my collarbones until they captured the delicate silver chain hanging between my breasts. Tugging the necklace free from my shirt, the four-carat diamond and accompanying wedding band caught the light. Declan positioned them neatly against my top, his fingers lingering across my breasts.

"Are you really okay?"

I smiled up at him, my hands capturing his and pressing them tighter to my chest. "Take me home so I can prove it."

"Wife. So demanding." But I could see his emerald eyes darken.

I threaded my fingers through his, tugging him towards the car. This chapter in my life was closed now. Once and for all.

And I couldn't wait to begin the next. For the girl who thought her fairy tale story would end in heartbreak, I was looking down at the beginning of what I knew was my happily ever after.

"You love it," I teased.

Declan slowed, pulling me around to bring my body against his, my belly, our future, safely tucked between us. His voice was soft, deep, as he pressed a kiss to my hair. "I love you."

"Always," I responded, turning my lips up for another.

Happily ever after indeed.

The End

OTHER BOOKS BY GENNI BEE

Steamy Shorts (Trio #1)
His to Have

His to Hold

With His Ring

Steamy Shorts (Trio #2)
His to Love

His to Protect

His to Keep

Public Relations Series
The Playboy Project

The Unplanned Project

The Practice Project

The Protection Project (coming fall 2023)

Kismet Series
New Year's Kismet

Could Be Kismet (coming early 2023)

ACKNOWLEDGEMENTS

A huge thank you to all my readers and those who have enjoyed my stories.

KEEP IN TOUCH

Like her Facebook Page
Find her on TikTok
Follow her on Instagram
Follow her on Amazon
Follow her on Bookbub

ABOUT THE AUTHOR

Genni Bee lives in the Midwest with her spouse, two awesome kids, and a cat who thinks he's a dog. She loves swoon-worthy, dirty-talking heros and heroines who know what they want.

A note from the author:

Nothing would be possible without the immense help that I received from my friends, my family, my wonderful beta readers (especially W.C. who has been with me since book) and a team of very patient editors. Thank you all.

Don't ever quit,
Genni Bee

Printed in Great Britain
by Amazon

18500086R00058